THE VELVETEEN RABBIT

ABRIDGED

MARGERY WILLIAMS
ILLUSTRATED BY GRAHAM PERCY

There was once a velveteen rabbit. He was fat and bunchy, as a rabbit should be; his coat was spotted, he had real thread whiskers, and his ears were lined with pink sateen. In the top of the Boy's Christmas stocking, with a sprig of holly between his paws, the effect was charming.

For at least two hours the Boy loved him, and then Aunts and Uncles came to dinner, and there was a great rustling of tissue paper and unwrapping of parcels, and in the excitement the Velveteen Rabbit was forgotten.

7

For a long time, he lived in the toy cupboard or on the nursery floor and no one thought very much about him. He was naturally shy, and being only made of velveteen, some of the more expensive toys quite snubbed him. Between them all the poor little Rabbit was made to feel himself very insignificant and commonplace, and the only person who was kind to him at all was the Skin Horse.

The Skin Horse had lived longer in the nursery than any of the others. He was wise, for he had seen a long succession of mechanical toys arrive to boast and swagger, and by-and-by break their mainsprings and pass away, and he knew that they were only toys, and would never turn into anything else. For nursery magic is very strange and wonderful, and only those playthings that are old and wise and experienced like the Skin Horse understand all about it.

'What is REAL?' asked the Rabbit one day, when they were lying side by side near the nursery fender.

'Real is a thing that happens to you,' answered the Skin Horse. 'When a child loves you for a long, long time, not just to play with, but REALLY loves you, then you become Real. It doesn't happen all at once. It takes a long time. Generally, by the time you are Real, most of your hair has been loved off, and your eyes drop out and you get loose in the joints and very shabby. But these things don't matter at all, because once you are Real you can't be ugly, except to people who don't understand.'

The Rabbit sighed. He longed to become Real; and yet the idea of growing shabby and losing his eyes and whiskers was rather sad.

One evening, when the Boy was going to bed, he couldn't find the china dog that always slept with him. Nana, who ruled the nursery, was in a hurry, so she simply looked about her, and seeing that the toy cupboard door stood open, 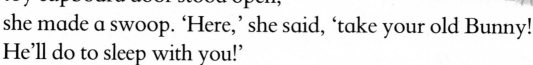 she made a swoop. 'Here,' she said, 'take your old Bunny! He'll do to sleep with you!'

That night, and for many nights after, the Velveteen Rabbit slept in the Boy's bed.

At first he found it rather uncomfortable, for the Boy hugged him very tight, and sometimes he rolled over him, and sometimes he pushed him so far under the pillow that the Rabbit could scarcely breathe.

But very soon he grew to like it, for the Boy used to talk to him, and made nice tunnels for him under the bedclothes. And when the Boy dropped off to sleep, the Rabbit would snuggle down close under his little warm chin and dream, with the Boy's hands clasped close round him all night long.

And so time went on, and the little Rabbit was so happy that he never noticed how his beautiful velveteen fur was getting shabbier and his tail coming unsewn, and all the pink rubbed off his nose where the Boy had kissed him.

Spring came, and they had long days in the garden, for wherever the Boy went the Rabbit went too. Once, when the Boy was called away suddenly to go out to tea, the Rabbit was left out on the lawn until long after dusk and Nana had to come and look for him with the candle because the Boy couldn't go to sleep unless he was there.

Nana grumbled as she rubbed him off with the corner of her apron. 'Fancy all that fuss for a toy!' she said.

The boy sat up in bed and stretched out his hands. 'Give me my Bunny!' he said. 'You mustn't say that. He isn't a toy. He's REAL!'

When the little Rabbit heard that, he was happy, for he knew that what the Skin Horse had said was true at last. He was Real. That night he was almost too happy to sleep, and so much love stirred in his little sawdust heart that it almost burst.

15

That was a wonderful Summer! Near the house where they lived there was a wood, and the Boy liked to go there after tea to play. He took the Velveteen Rabbit with him and he always made the Rabbit a little nest somewhere among the bracken, where he would be quite cosy.

One evening, while the Rabbit was lying there alone, he saw two strange beings creep out of the tall bracken near him. They were rabbits like himself, but quite furry and brand-new and they changed shape in a queer way when they moved instead of always staying the same like he did.

One came quite close but he wrinkled his nose suddenly and jumped backwards. 'He doesn't smell right!' he exclaimed. 'He isn't a rabbit at all! He isn't real!'

'I AM Real!' said the little Rabbit. 'I am Real! The Boy said so!' And he nearly began to cry.

Just then the Boy ran past near them, and with a flash of white tails the two strange rabbits disappeared.

'Come back and play with me!' called the little Rabbit. 'Oh, do come back! I KNOW I am Real.' For a long time he lay very still, hoping that they would come back. But they never returned, and presently the sun sank lower and the little white moths fluttered out, and the Boy came and carried him home.

Weeks passed, and the little Rabbit grew very old and shabby. The Boy loved him so hard that he loved all his whiskers off, and the pink lining to his ears turned grey, and his brown spots faded. He scarcely looked like a rabbit any more, except to the Boy.

And then one day the Boy was ill. His face grew very flushed and his little body was so hot that it burned the Rabbit when he held him close. Strange people came and went in the nursery, and through it all the little Velveteen Rabbit lay there, hidden from sight under the bedclothes, for he was afraid that if they found him someone might take him away, and he knew that the Boy needed him.

It was a long weary time, for the Boy was too ill to play. But the Rabbit snuggled down patiently, and looked forward to the time when the Boy should be well again.

Presently the fever turned, and the boy got better. And one day, they let him get up and dress. They carried the Boy out on to the balcony, wrapped in a shawl, and the little Rabbit lay tangled up among the bedclothes, thinking.

The boy was going to the seaside tomorrow. Everything was arranged, and now it only remained to carry out the doctor's orders. The room was to be disinfected, and all the books and toys that the Boy had played with in bed must be burnt.

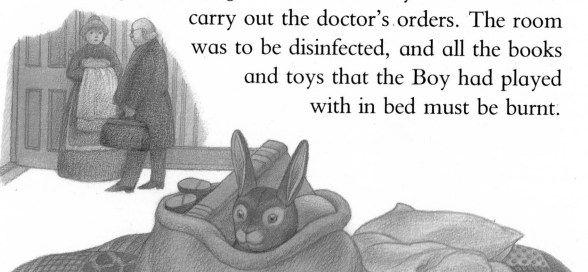

Just then Nana caught sight of him. 'How about this old Bunny?' she asked.

'THAT?' said the doctor. 'Why, it's a mass of scarlet fever germs! – Burn it at once. Get him a new one. He mustn't have that any more.'

And so the little Rabbit was put into a sack with the old picture-books and a lot of rubbish, and carried out to the end of the garden behind the fowl-house.

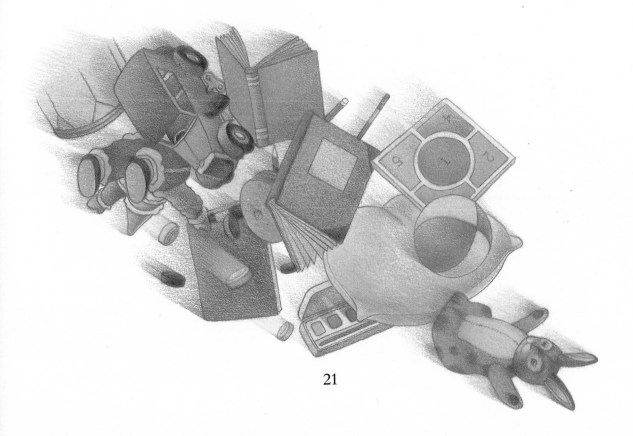

That night the Boy slept in a different bedroom, and he had a new bunny to sleep with him. It was a splendid bunny, all white plush with real glass eyes, but the Boy was too excited to care very much about it.

And while the Boy was asleep, dreaming of the seaside, the little Rabbit lay among the old picture-books in the corner behind the fowl-house, and he felt very lonely. He thought of those long sunlit hours in the garden – how happy they were – and a great sadness came over him. And a tear, a real tear, trickled down his little shabby velvet nose and fell to the ground.

And then a strange thing happened. For where the tear had fallen, a flower grew out of the ground and out of it there stepped a fairy. She came close to the little Rabbit and kissed him on his velveteen nose. 'I am the nursery magic Fairy,' she said. 'I take care of all the playthings that the children have loved. When they are old and worn out and the children don't need them any more, then I come and take them away with me and turn them into Real.'

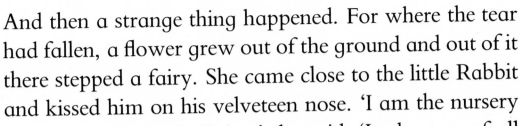

'Wasn't I Real before?'
asked the little Rabbit.

'You were Real to the
Boy,' the Fairy said, 'because he
loved you. Now you shall be Real to
everyone.' And she held the little Rabbit
close in her arms and flew with him into the wood.

In the open glade between the tree-trunks the wild
rabbits danced with their shadows on the velvet grass.

'I've brought you a new playfellow,' the fairy said. And
she kissed the little Rabbit again and put him down
on the grass.

The little Rabbit sat quite still for a moment and never moved. For when he saw all the wild rabbits dancing around him he didn't want them to see that he was made all in one piece. He did not know that when the Fairy kissed him that last time she had changed him altogether. Just then something tickled his nose, and before he thought what he was doing he lifted his hind toe to scratch it.

And he found that he actually had hind legs! Instead of dingy velveteen he had brown fur, soft and shiny, his ears twitched by themselves, and his whiskers were so long that they brushed the grass. He gave one leap and the joy of using his hind legs was so great that he went springing about the turf on them. He was a Real Rabbit at last!

Autumn passed and Winter, and in the Spring, when the days grew warm and sunny, the Boy went out to play in the wood. And while he was playing, two rabbits crept out from the bracken and peeped at him. One had strange markings under his fur, as though long ago he had been spotted, and the spots still showed through. And about his little soft nose and his round black eyes there was something familiar.

'Why, he looks just like my old Bunny that was lost when I had scarlet fever!' the Boy thought. But he never knew that it really was his own Bunny, come back to look at the child who had first helped him to be Real.

First published in 1922 by William Heinemann Limited

This edition first published in 1987 by
Treasure Press
59 Grosvenor Street
London W1

© Copyright this edition 1987 Octopus Books Limited

ISBN 1 85051 257 4

Printed in the United Kingdom